The Tiara Club

at Ruby Mansions

For Princess Sophie,
and Princess Isabelle too xxx
VF

www.tiaraclub.co.uk

ORCHARD BOOKS
338 Euston Road, London NW1 3BH
Orchard Books Australia
Level 17/207 Kent St, Sydney, NSW 2000

A Paperback Original
First published in Great Britain in 2007
Text © Vivian French 2007
Illustrations © Orchard Books 2007
The right of Vivian French to be identified as the author of this
work has been asserted by her in accordance with Copyright,
Designs and Patents Act, 1988.

A CIP catalogue record for this book is available
from the British Library.

ISBN 978 1 84616 295 4

1 3 5 7 9 10 8 6 4 2

Printed in Great Britain

The paper and board used in this paperback are natural
recyclable products made from wood grown in sustainable
forests. The manufacturing processes conform to the
environmental regulations of the country of origin.

Orchard Books is a division of Hachette Children's Books
www.orchardbooks.co.uk

The Tiara Club
at Ruby Mansions

Princess Amy

and the Golden Coach

By Vivian French

ORCHARD BOOKS

The Royal Palace Academy
for the Preparation of Perfect Princesses

(Known to our students as "*The Princess Academy*")

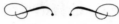

OUR SCHOOL MOTTO:
A Perfect Princess always thinks of others
before herself, and is kind, caring and truthful.

Ruby Mansions offers a complete education for
Tiara Club princesses with emphasis on the
creative arts. The curriculum includes:

Innovative Ideas for our
Friendship Festival

Ballet for Grace
and Poise

Designing Floral
Bouquets
(all thorns will be
removed)

A visit to the Diamond
Exhibition
(on the joyous occasion of
Queen Fabiola's birthday)

Our headteacher, Queen Fabiola, is present at all times,
and students are well looked after by the head fairy
godmother, Fairy G, and her assistant, Fairy Angora.

Our resident staff and visiting experts include:

KING BERNARDO IV
(Ruby Mansions Governor)

LADY HARRIS
(Secretary to Queen Fabiola)

LADY ARAMINTA
(Princess Academy Matron)

QUEEN MOTHER MATILDA
(Etiquette, Posture and
Flower Arranging)

We award tiara points to encourage our Tiara Club princesses towards the next level. All princesses who win enough points at Ruby Mansions will attend a celebration ball, where they will be presented with their Ruby Sashes.

Ruby Sash Tiara Club princesses are invited to go on to Pearl Palace, our very special residence for Perfect Princesses, where they may continue their education at a higher level.

PLEASE NOTE:
Princesses are expected to arrive at
the Academy with a *minimum* of:

TWENTY BALLGOWNS
(with all necessary hoops,
petticoats, etc)

TWELVE DAY DRESSES

SEVEN GOWNS
suitable for garden parties,
and other special
day occasions

TWELVE TIARAS

DANCING SHOES
five pairs

VELVET SLIPPERS
three pairs

RIDING BOOTS
two pairs

Cloaks, muffs, stoles, gloves
and other essential
accessories as required

Hello to all princesses – especially you!
I'm Princess Amy, from Poppy Room.
Don't you just LOVE being here at Ruby
Mansions? Although I'm sure Pearl Palace
will be HUGE fun – just as long as you're
there, and all my other friends from Poppy
Room too. I couldn't do without Chloe,
Jessica, Georgia, Olivia and Lauren.
I wonder if the horrible twins, Diamonde
and Gruella, will be at Pearl Palace?
Ooooh! They're SO mean!
Especially Diamonde...

"One two three TWIRL! One two three TWIRL!"

Fairy Angora waved her wand in time to the music. We did our best to follow her instructions, but it wasn't easy. I kept getting dizzy, and bumping into my friends.

"Please, Fairy Angora – couldn't you help us with a bit of magic?"

As I spoke I found I'd twirled myself into a corner and had to come out backwards. "I'm SO not good at ballet!"

Fairy Angora (she's the assistant fairy godmother at the Princess Academy) laughed. "That would be cheating, my angel," she said.

"Ballet teaches you grace and poise. If I did it by magic it would fade away, and then what would happen at tomorrow's end-of-term dancing display?"

Diamonde sniggered. "Amy will be stamping about like a big fat elephant!"

Fairy Angora gave her a frosty look. "That, Diamonde, is not a kind or helpful thing to say. Please show us your very best pirouette."

Diamonde looked so horribly pleased with herself as she stepped forward.

"Certainly, Fairy Angora," she said, and she did three perfect pirouettes one after the other, ending with the most beautiful curtsey. We couldn't help bursting into a massive round of applause – she was REALLY good. Of course Diamonde looked more smug than ever.

"Well done, Diamonde," Fairy

Angora said, but she didn't sound as pleased as she usually does when one of us does something right. "I can see you've had lots of lessons. You may have two tiara points." And she went to talk to the musicians.

"Diamonde and I have been going to ballet since we were three," Gruella told us. "Mummy says it's SO important that princesses like us have EVERY opportunity to learn to be graceful."

"That's right!" Diamonde gave me a snooty look. "I don't suppose YOUR parents thought such things mattered, and that's why you're so hopeless."

I stared at her in absolute amazement. "You don't know anything about my parents!" I said. "How can you say such things? If you really want to know, I did go to ballet when I was little, but..." I hesitated. Did I really want Diamonde and Gruella to know about my family? But then I thought, *Hey! I'm proud of my Mum and Dad!* So I went on. "But the lessons were too expensive.

They've hardly got ANY money, but they always want me to have the best. Why, they even cancelled a wonderful Royal Tour so I could come here in their very special travelling coach!"

Diamonde stuck her nose in the air. "Huh! I saw you arrive! THAT wasn't a very special coach. Why, it wasn't even gold. Didn't you know that Perfect Princesses ALWAYS travel in GOLDEN coaches?"

Luckily for me, Fairy Angora came hurrying back just then – otherwise I would have said something that would NOT have been at all princessy.

"Did I hear you mention a golden coach?" she asked, and she looked very anxious. "Oh no! Has somebody told you Queen Fabiola's secret?"

Of course we all shook our heads – except for Diamonde.

She winked at Gruella and said, "Well...someone might have told us about a very special coach..."

It was SO obvious she didn't really know anything, but Fairy Angora didn't seem to notice. She sat down on a chair looking very upset. "Queen Fabiola will be furious! She wanted it to be such a wonderful surprise! The most beautiful golden coach you've ever seen to take you to the end-of-term celebration ball!"

Chapter Two

We didn't know what to say. Fairy Angora had just told us our headteacher's secret, and we weren't meant to know!

Gruella put her hand up. "How will we all fit into one coach?" she asked. "And why isn't the ball going to be here – OUCH!" She turned and glared at Diamonde.

"Why did you pinch me?"

"Sssssh!" Diamonde hissed, but she was too late. Fairy Angora was staring at her, her eyes wide.

"You DIDN'T know about the queen's secret surprise, did you, Diamonde? Because if someone really HAD told you, you'd know the ball was going to be at Pearl Palace. And you'd know that only the very best dancers will be travelling in the golden coach! You were just pretending you knew!"

Diamonde shuffled her feet. "I only said someone MIGHT have told us," she muttered.

Fairy Angora clutched her wand. "Oh – how SILLY I am." She looked round at us all, and her cheeks were very pink.

"Please, my angels, PLEASE try
and forget what I said. We want
our princesses to always try
their best, not just because they
want to win a place in
a wonderful coach."

"It's all right, Fairy Angora,"
Olivia said. "We won't even think

about the coach." And we all nodded...except for Diamonde.

She gave Fairy Angora SUCH a sly look. "If we pretend we don't know about this coach," she said, "will we get extra tiara points for ballet?"

"That's right!" Gruella agreed.

"LOTS of tiara points so we're sure to ride in the coach!"

I was so shocked! We all know that Perfect Princesses never EVER talk like that.

And Fairy Angora went positively pale – but then she folded her arms, and frowned.

"Princess Diamonde and Princess Gruella," she said, "just this once I will overlook the way you have spoken to me, because I should never have asked you to keep a secret." She stopped, and looked at me. "Amy, would you be an angel and run along to Fairy G's office? Please ask her if I can borrow her Forgetting Dust." She turned back to the class. "I'll sprinkle a little in this room, and all of you will forget what I have said. That way none of us will need to worry about tiara points and the golden coach. And now, let's go back to our ballet lesson."

As I hurried out of the door I saw Diamonde and Gruella looking SO disappointed.

Fairy G is the head fairy godmother, and she has offices all over the Princess Academy. Her room in Ruby Mansions was at the end of a long marble corridor, and the maids were busy polishing the floor as I walked up to her door and knocked.

"Come in!" she called, and I went inside.

Fairy G was sitting behind her desk knitting something ruby red and sparkly. She saw me looking, and smiled. "It's a shawl to wear to the Celebration Ball," she explained. "For when you're presented with your Ruby Sashes. What can I do for you, Amy dear?"

I curtsied, and told her that Fairy Angora needed to borrow some Forgetting Dust. Fairy G's eyebrows zoomed up, but all she said was, "Of course. You'll find it over there on the shelf – the yellow bottle."

Fairy G's shelves were absolutely stuffed with jars and bags and bottles. I think she must have used magic to find what she wanted, because they were SO untidy and higgledy piggledy.

When I reached up and took the yellow bottle off the shelf, a collection of odd-looking twigs and dried flowers nearly fell on top of me, but at the last minute Fairy G waved her wand, and they flew back to the place they'd come from.

"Tell Fairy Angora to use the dust carefully, Amy," Fairy G said. "It's powerful stuff! And remind her it only lasts a day or two."

"Yes, Fairy G," I said. "Thank you very much!"

The marble corridor was gleaming as I came out of Fairy G's room. The maids had gone, but the floor was still a little bit wet. I walked very carefully, and I'd SO nearly got back to our classroom when I sneezed – and I don't know how it happened, but my feet slid from under me. I grabbed at the door to save myself, and dropped the yellow bottle – and it crashed to the floor and broke into a million little pieces.

Chapter Three

"Oh NO..." I wailed. "Oh no..."

I didn't know WHAT to do. I stared at the mess in horror, my heart thudding in my chest – and then the strangest feeling crept into my head. It felt like fog in my brain...and I couldn't remember where I was, and why I was looking at lots of yellow powder and broken glass spread in front of me.

The door beside me opened, and Fairy Angora popped her head out.

"Amy!" she said. "What was

that crash? Are you all right?" And then she saw the mess. "Is that the Forgetting Dust? Quick! Come inside—" She grabbed my hand and pulled me into the classroom.

As she slammed the door behind me a little cloud of yellow powder flew into the air, and the foggy feeling in my head grew stronger.

"Amy! Amy?" Fairy Angora waved her wand over my head. "Do you know who I am?"

It was SO weird! I knew I knew her name – but I just COULDN'T think what it was! "Erm..." I began. "Erm... I'm so sorry..."

"Oooh! What's the matter with Amy?" asked a spiteful voice. "Has she gone mad?"

I rubbed my head furiously. I knew who had spoken, but I couldn't remember her name either. Was I REALLY going mad?

Fairy Angora tapped my shoulder twice with her wand, and said, "Forgetting Dust, your task is done. Please leave Amy – three two ONE!"

My head cleared at once.

"THANK YOU, Fairy Angora,"
I said. "I'm so VERY sorry
I dropped the bottle. Should I get
a dustpan and brush?"

Fairy Angora shook her head.

"Even though I've taken the spell away, you'd forget what you were doing after a second or two. Don't worry about it, my angel. Anyone can have an accident."

The spiteful voice, and I knew now that it belonged to Diamonde, "If you ask me, only CLUMSY people fall over and drop precious spells!"

Gruella sniggered. "Clumsy people like elephant Amy!"

"Diamonde! Gruella!" Fairy Angora was really cross. "I've had QUITE enough of your nasty little comments! Kindly go and sit in the corner until I say you can get up again." She watched the twins stamp across to the chairs in the corner, then turned to the rest of us. "I'm very sorry, my petals, but I'll have to ask you to stay in this room until the Forgetting Dust is cleared away from outside. And don't go near the door, either. I'll set you a task, and then I'll fetch Fairy G to help me tidy it up. Now – let's try those pirouettes again, shall we? Ready? One two three TWIRL!"

And the most AMAZING thing happened! I found myself spinning across the room as if I'd been doing ballet all my life!

It was SO strange! As I came to a
halt on the other side of the room
Fairy Angora clapped her hands.

"Well DONE, Amy!" she said. "That was WONDERFUL! Five tiara points!"

There was a loud angry snort from Diamonde, and Gruella whispered, "That's SO not fair! You only got two points!"

"I know. And I bet it's the magic dust that's making Amy do that," Diamonde hissed back.

Fairy Angora overheard her. "Actually, Diamonde – it isn't magic. Sometimes when you clear away Forgetting Dust it makes your memory sharper. Did you do ballet when you were little, Amy?"

I nodded.

Fairy Angora beamed. "That'll be the reason, then. You're just remembering an old skill! Now, please get into groups. I'd like you to work out a lovely dance sequence while I run and fetch Fairy G, and after we've

taken the magic dust away I'll ask her to watch you dancing."

Of course all of us Poppy Roomers hurried together to make a group, and as usual Diamonde and Gruella decided they were going to work together.

Fairy Angora waited until she saw we were busy, and then carefully opened the door and slipped out.

As the door closed Diamonde hurried towards it, pulling Gruella behind her. "I want some of that magic powder!" she said. "I just KNOW that's what made stupid Amy dance like that—" She bent down, opened the door, and scooped as much Forgetting Dust as she could from the floor. With a huge smile she put her fingers to her nose, and sniffed hard...

Chapter Four

It was SO weird!

Diamonde blinked, sneezed, and said in a squeaky voice, "Where am I?"

Gruella stared at her. "Don't be silly, Diamonde," she said. "You're in a ballet lesson!"

"Ballet?" Diamonde clapped her hands. "Ooooh! I LOVE ballet!"

And she hopped and thumped across the floor as if she was a little toddler.

"DIAMONDE!" Gruella sounded really quite frightened. "Stop it!"

Lauren shook her head. "I don't think she can stop," she said. "I think it's the Forgetting Dust working. She's forgotten how old she is!"

"But she can't keep behaving like a two-year-old!" Gruella gasped. "We'll NEVER get any extra tiara points if she can't dance properly!"

"La di di dee, la di di dee!" Diamonde sang, and she did a little twirl and fell over. She sat on the floor and laughed. "Silly billy me! Diamonde did go all fall down!"

"I'm sure Fairy Angora will be

able to take the spell off again."
Georgia said hopefully. "She did
with Amy."

"But she'll be FURIOUS with
Diamonde!" Gruella wailed. "She
told us not to go near the door!
And we've just GOT to get some
more tiara points, or we won't
win our Ruby Sashes tomorrow
and get to go to Pearl Palace in
the golden coach!"

I looked at Diamonde, who was
sitting on the floor sucking her
thumb. It was odd, but I couldn't
help feeling just a little bit sorry
for her and Gruella. I know the
twins are absolutely horrible most

of the time, but they do care about each other.

"Do you know what?" I said slowly. "I might just have an idea...."

"Do you REALLY?" Gruella's eyes lit up. "Oh, Amy! If you help us I PROMISE I'll be nice to you for ever and ever!"

"Well," I began, "it depends if the rest of Poppy Room are willing to help..."

"Of COURSE we are!" Georgia sounded most indignant. "You know we will, Amy!"

"That's right!" Jessica nodded hard. "Poppy Room to the rescue!"

I smiled my thanks, and went on, "Supposing we did a dance where we all pretended that Diamonde was PRETENDING to be a little girl? And we were teaching her all the different ballet steps? That way we'd get to show off what we could do, and maybe Fairy Angora and Fairy G won't notice she's under a spell until it wears off. Fairy G told me it only lasts a day."

All my friends and Gruella gazed at me. "AMY!" Chloe said. "That's SO brilliant! How DID you think of it? It's perfect!"

I could feel myself blushing. "Thanks very much," I mumbled. "Erm...shall we get started?"

By the time Fairy Angora came back with Fairy G we'd worked out a whole dance routine. I don't want to sound boastful, but it worked better than I'd even dared to hope! We showed Diamonde the different steps, and she laughed and clapped her hands, and did her best to copy us EXACTLY as if she was about two years old. It was actually really good fun – Diamonde was so sweet! And Gruella was lovely too, although we did keep having to tell her not to look so worried.

We knew when the two fairy godmothers were outside because we heard Fairy G's huge voice booming, "Forgetting Dust upon the ground, back in the bottle, safe and sound!"

There was a bright yellow flash, and then the door opened, and Fairy G sailed in with the bottle in her hand looking as if it had never been broken. Fairy Angora floated behind her smiling happily.

"There, my angels!" she said. "All better! And now show us what you've been doing!"

We were the last to show our dance, and it was a bit difficult while we were waiting because Diamonde kept whispering, "Want a bickie! Want some juice!" Luckily we managed to keep her quiet, although I did wonder if Fairy G was peering in our direction once or twice.

When we came to show off our routine though, Diamonde was WONDERFUL! Fairy G and Fairy Angora clapped and clapped, and we were given

FIFTEEN tiara points each!

"Well done!" Fairy Angora was positively glowing, she was so pleased. "And I'm SO happy that you've worked so hard, Diamonde. You've more than made up for your bad behaviour earlier."

"Yes! Tank 'oo, nice fairy!" And before we could stop her, Diamonde rushed forward and gave Fairy Angora a huge hug. "I is a GOOD girl!" she said as she fluttered her eyelashes madly. "I is PRETTY Princess Diamonde! Tee hee heee!" And she twirled round and round the room until she fell over again, and sat laughing at us.

Chapter Five

"Diamonde!" Fairy Angora didn't look very pleased. "You don't need to go on pretending now, you know."

And Fairy G didn't look very happy either. She folded her arms, and looked stern. "I'm sorry to tell you, Fairy Angora, but Diamonde ISN'T pretending!

It seems to me there's been some very clever thinking here to cover up the use of the Forgetting Dust. WHO is responsible for this?"

My heart began to pitter-pat in my chest, but I had to step forward. "Please, Fairy G – it was me..."

But all of a sudden the most EXTRAORDINARY thing happened. Diamonde smiled and pulled herself to her feet, and said, "Amy is a GOOD girl, big fairy! It was me what did play with the fairy dust." She put her head on one side, and rolled her eyes.

"Diamonde is a BAD girl." And she slapped her own wrist, and giggled.

There was a long silence...and then Fairy G began to laugh. She laughed and she laughed, and before long we were all laughing too – even Gruella and Diamonde.

"You know," Fairy G said as she wiped her streaming eyes, "we don't need a competition tomorrow. "I know EXACTLY who should ride in Queen Fabiola's Golden Coach, and lead the cavalcade to Pearl Palace. Princess Amy – you're a STAR! And so are all of Poppy Room – and, I'm delighted to say, Gruella as well. And I hope Diamonde will appreciate just how generous you've been, and how very VERY kind."

Fairy Angora nodded. "Should we take the Forgetting Dust away?" she asked.

Fairy G stroked her chin thoughtfully. "I think perhaps we should," she said. "Forgetting Dust, your task is done. Leave Diamonde, three two ONE!"

Tiny yellow sparkles filled the air, and Diamonde rubbed her eyes and yawned as if she'd just woken up. She looked round at us all, and smiled – a really lovely smile.

"Hello," she said. "I've just had the STRANGEST dream... I dreamt I was little, and you were all being SO sweet to me! Thank you!"

Olivia nudged me. "Do you think she might have forgotten how to be mean?" she whispered.

"I don't know," I whispered back. "Let's just enjoy it while it lasts."

And we did. Diamonde went on being lovely for all of the rest of the day, and the next day too. When we rode in the GLORIOUS golden coach to Pearl Palace she insisted I sat in the very best seat.

As we lined up in front of Queen Fabiola to receive our Ruby Sashes she told our headteacher that I was the nicest girl in the whole of the Princess Academy.

As the music began for the celebration ball she curtsied to me, and said, "Amy – I know I've sometimes been mean to you – but can we be friends? REAL friends?"

And I smiled at her, and said,
"Of course we can!" And I really
truly meant it...but I couldn't help
noticing that as the evening went
on she tried harder and HARDER
to be the best at every dance.

When she pushed Georgia out of the way so she could take the biggest helping of strawberry jelly I knew the spell had finally worn off...but it had been nice while it lasted.

And as I snuggled down in Poppy Room that night I thought, I've got so many really WONDERFUL friends that I don't mind if Diamonde and Gruella are sometimes horrible. There's Chloe, and Olivia, and Georgia and Lauren and Jessica – and best of all, there's YOU!

And we're all going to be together again very VERY soon – because next term we'll all be at Pearl Palace... So HURRAH for the Tiara Club!

What happens next in
Pearl Palace?
Meet the Lily Room princesses in:

Princess Hannah
and the **Little Black Kitten**

Princess Isabella
and the **Snow-White Unicorn**

Princess Lucy
and the **Precious Puppy**

Princess Grace
and the **Golden Nightingale**

Princess Ellie
and the **Enchanted Fawn**

Princess Sarah
and the **Silver Swan**

Win a Tiara Club
Perfect Princess Prize!

Look for the secret word in mirror writing that is
hidden in a tiara in each of the Tiara Club books.
Each book has one word. Put together the six words
from books **13** to **18** to make a special Perfect
Princess sentence, then send it to us together with
20 words or more on why you like the Tiara Club
books. Each month, we will put the correct entries
in a draw and one lucky reader will receive a magical
Perfect Princess prize!

Send your Perfect Princess sentence,
at least 20 words on why you like the Tiara Club,
your name and your address on a postcard to:
The Tiara Club Competition,
Orchard Books, 338 Euston Road,
London, NW1 3BH

Australian readers should write to:
Hachette Children's Books,
Level 17/207 Kent Street, Sydney, NSW 2000.

Only one entry per child.
Final draw: 31 May 2008

The Tiara Club

By Vivian French
Illustrated by Sarah Gibb
The Tiara Club

The Tiara Club at Silver Towers

The Tiara Club at Ruby Mansions

All priced at £3.99.
Christmas Wonderland and *Butterfly Ball* are priced at £5.99.
The Tiara Club books are available from all good bookshops, or can be ordered direct
from the publisher: Orchard Books, PO BOX 29, Douglas IM99 1BQ.
Credit card orders please telephone 01624 836000 or fax 01624 837033 or visit our
website: www.wattspub.co.uk or e-mail: bookshop@enterprise.net for details.

To order please quote title, author, ISBN and your full name and address.
Cheques and postal orders should be made payable to 'Bookpost plc.'
Postage and packing is FREE within the UK
(overseas customers should add £2.00 per book).

Prices and availability are subject to change.

Look out for

Butterfly Ball

with Princess Amy and Princess Olivia!
ISBN 978 1 84616 470 5

Check out

website at:

www.tiaraclub.co.uk

You'll find Perfect Princess games and fun
things to do, as well as news on the Tiara
Club and all your favourite princesses!